# The Hanukkah Mice

by **Steven Kroll**  illustrated by **Michelle Shapiro**

AMAZON CHILDREN'S PUBLISHING

Amazon Publishing
Attn: Amazon Children's Publishing
P.O. Box 400818
Las Vegas, NV 89149
www.amazon.com/amazonchildrenspublishing

Library of Congress Cataloging-in-Publication Data

Kroll, Steven.
The Hanukkah mice / by Steven Kroll ; illustrated by Michelle Shapiro. —
1st ed.
p. cm.
Summary: A family of mice enjoys the dollhouse and furnishings that
Rachel receives as gifts on the eight nights of Hanukkah.
ISBN 978-0-7614-5428-1 (hardcover) 978-0-7614-5988-0 (paperback)
[1. Mice—Fiction.  2. Hanukkah—Fiction.]  I. Shapiro, Michelle, 1961-
ill.  II. Title.
PZ7.K9225Ham 2008
[E]—dc22
2007035003

Book design by Becky Terhune
Editor: Margery Cuyler

Printed in China (W)
10 9 8 7 6 5 4 3 2 1

**For Kathleen**
—S. K.


**For Andrea and Natalie**
—M. S.

It was the first night of Hanukkah. The mouse family scampered out of their mouse hole and up the basement stairs.

They watched Mr. Silman, one of the Big People,
lift the shammes candle, say the prayers, and light
the first Hanukkah candle.

"Now it's time for Rachel to open her first Hanukkah gift," he said. Rachel couldn't wait. She unwrapped the big box in the middle of the living room.

She gasped at what she saw, an exquisitely carved dollhouse with a porch and white trim that wrapped around the outside like the frosting on a wedding cake. Each window had a set of tiny lace curtains in it.

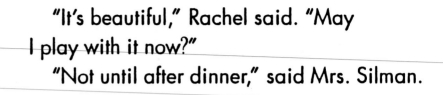

"It's beautiful," Rachel said. "May I play with it now?"

"Not until after dinner," said Mrs. Silman.

Mindy Mouse tugged her little brother's tail.
"Mitchell, it's just the right size for us," she whispered.
"Yeah, you're right," said Mitchell.

The mouse family watched the Silmans eat their holiday supper.

They watched Rachel play with the dollhouse after dessert.

They scurried behind Mr. Silman as he carried the dollhouse to Rachel's room.

They watched as Rachel finally fell asleep.

Then . . . Mindy poked Mitchell.
"Come on! Let's explore!"

"Shhh!" said Mama.
"Hurry!" said Papa.
The mice skittered inside
the dollhouse.
"This place would be really
cool if it had some furniture,"
said Mitchell.
"Look at me! I can do
somersaults!" said Mindy.

On the second night of Hanukkah,
the mouse family watched Mr. Silman
light the second candle.

Rachel opened another Hanukkah gift. It was a miniature wingback chair with a little matching stool.

"Just right for tiny feet!" said Rachel.

When the mouse family visited the dollhouse
later that night, the wing chair was sitting in
the living room. Papa settled into it with a smile.

On the third night, Rachel's gift was a little sofa.
She laughed. "Just right for a tiny family!"
And sure enough, later that night the mouse family
found it next to the wingback chair.
"Look at me!" said Mindy, bouncing up and down
on the cushions as Mitchell threw a pillow at her.

On the fourth night, Rachel got a set of little plates.
"Just right for tiny latkes!" she said.
When the mouse family saw the plates later,
they had tiny latkes with applesauce on them.

"Yum!" said Mitchell.
"I wonder where those latkes
came from," Mama said.

On the fifth night, there was a bureau in the bedroom with some Hanukkah gelt . . .

and on the sixth night, two beds appeared, each with a dreidel on the pillow.

"Hey!" said Mindy, giving one a spin.

"Wow!" said Mitchell, spinning the other.
"I wonder where all this came from," said Mama.

Then, on night number seven, Rachel's gift was a table and chairs. The mouse family found them right in the middle of the dollhouse dining room. The table was covered with a special Hanukkah cloth.

"I wonder where that tablecloth came from," said Mama.

On the last night of Hanukkah, Rachel's eighth gift was a new, miniature menorah.

"Perfect!" she said.

When the menorah turned up on the dollhouse dining table, together with a festive holiday meal, the mouse family gathered around.

"Our very own menorah for our very own
Hanukkah," said Papa, "and so much wonderful food!"
He lit all eight electric candles and said the prayers.
"Happy Hanukkah!" said Mindy and Mitchell.
"Happy Hanukkah!" said Papa.
"I wonder where all this came from," said Mama.

And from under the covers,
Rachel smiled.